The Culvert Spaceship

Adventure Mars

By Pamela J. Mulliken

ISBN:

E-Book: 978-1-966131-56-4
Paperback: 978-1-966131-57-1
Hardcover: 978-1-966131-58-8

Dedication

I lovingly dedicate this book to my husband, Jack, whose unwavering support and encouragement inspire me every day. Thank you for standing by me through all my wild ideas and projects.

About the Author

Pamela Mulliken is a retired educator with 29 years of teaching experience across kindergarten to 12th grade, specializing in English as a second language, Spanish, Elementary education, and Special education. She holds a Bachelor of Science in Elementary Education, a Master of Science in Special Education, and numerous endorsements, including English as a second language and Art. A native of Nebraska, Pamela enjoys painting, drawing, gardening, and writing in her spare time. Her debut book marks the first installment in a series of planned sequels, combining non-fiction materials with engaging activities, vocabulary, and quizzes to enhance comprehension. Inspired by her quest for captivating activities to accompany the stories she read to her non-English speaking students, Pamela aims to provide educators and parents with valuable resources. Join Pamela on her literary journey as she endeavors to create enriching experiences for both teachers and students alike.

Table of Contents

CHAPTER 1: THE CULVERT ROCKET

Two weeks had passed since Mia, Eli, and Jack returned from their unbelievable journey to the moon. No one at school would believe them, of course. How could they? The trio had built their spaceship from an old culvert they found in the woods. To anyone else, it looked like a rusty metal pipe patched together with scrap parts. But to them, it was a portal to the stars.

"Are you sure we should go back?" Eli nervously asked, adjusting his glasses as the three stood before their makeshift rocket. The culvert gleamed faintly in the late afternoon sun, looking more mysterious than ever.

"Of course we should!" Mia replied, her long black hair catching the light. She was the boldest of the group, the one who always wanted to push the boundaries of adventure. "We have to figure out what happened last time."

Jack, the quiet but clever one, knelt down and inspected the base of the rocket. "It's just sitting here," he said, running his hand along the metal. "No scorch marks. No damage. You'd never guess it blasted us to the moon."

Exactly," Mia said, her voice dropping into a whisper. "Something about this ship… it's not normal."

Eli hesitated, glancing at the woods around them. The late summer air buzzed with the sound of cicadas, but the rocket felt out of place as if it didn't belong in their world at all. "What if it happens again?" he asked. "What if we… fall asleep?"

"That's why we're here," Mia said, already climbing the metal ladder leading to the cockpit. "To find out what this thing really is."

Jack gave Eli a reassuring nudge. "Come on. We'll stick together this time."

Reluctantly, Eli followed, and soon all three of them were crammed into the cockpit. It was just as they'd left it—crude metal walls, a control panel made of old circuit boards Jack had scavenged, and a single red button in the middle of the dashboard that none of them dared to press.

They sat quietly for a moment, the small cabin filling with the sound of their breathing. Then, without warning, a soft hum filled the air. The walls of the rocket seemed to vibrate as if the ship were alive.

"Do you hear that?" Jack whispered, his voice tinged with both fear and awe.

Mia opened her mouth to answer, but her eyes grew heavy before she could. Eli slumped back in his seat, and Jack's head drooped forward. Within seconds, all three were fast asleep.

MIA
JACK
ELI

CHAPTER 2: MARS BOUND

Mia's eyes fluttered open to the soft glow of orange light streaming through a small circular window. Her heart skipped as she realized they weren't in the woods anymore.

"Guys, wake up!" she shouted, shaking Eli and Jack awake. They jolted upright, their eyes wide as they saw before them.

Outside the window stretched a vast expanse of red soil and jagged rocks, with distant hills rising against a burnt-orange sky. A faint sun hung low on the horizon, casting long shadows over the alien terrain.

"This… this isn't the moon," Eli stammered, pressing his face to the glass. "Where are we?"

Jack pointed to a small screen on the control panel, where a single word blinked in green letters: MARS.

"No way," Mia breathed, her voice barely audible. "We're on Mars, and we're back in our space suits?"

Jack scrambled to check the controls, but as before, there were no switches or levers to steer the ship—just the strange red button that glowed faintly as if waiting for them to press it. "This thing brought us here," he said. "But why?"

Mia unlatched the hatch and pushed it open; a rush of red, dusty air swirled around her face. "I guess we're about to find out."

They climbed out of the rocket one by one and stepped onto the Martian surface. The ground crunched under their feet, a mix of fine red dust and rough pebbles. The air was eerily quiet, and the vastness of the landscape made them feel impossibly small.

"Look at this place," Eli said, his voice filled with awe. "It's… empty."

"Not completely," Mia said, pointing to a faint trail of marks in the dust. "Something's been here."

The three of them followed the trail cautiously, their footsteps leaving crisp prints in the Martian soil. They noticed something odd as they walked: the trail didn't seem random. It led in a straight line as if something—or someone—had a destination in mind.

What do you think made these?" Jack asked, crouching down to inspect the marks. "They're not footprints. Too wide."

Mia shook her head. "I don't know, but whatever it is, it's recent."

Eli glanced nervously back toward the rocket. "Should we really be going this far? What if we can't find our way back?"

"We have to," Mia said firmly. "If we want answers, we have to follow the trail."

Jack hesitated but nodded. "Mia's right. If this rocket brought us here, there has to be a reason."

The Martian mystery deepened with every step, and the three friends couldn't shake the feeling that they were being watched.

CHAPTER 3: THE RED TRAIL

The faint marks stretched across the Martian surface, leading the trio past jagged rocks and dips in the terrain.

"This is so weird," Mia said, squinting at the horizon. "Why would tracks just… stop and start like this?"

Jack crouched and traced the dusty marks with his finger. "They're too big to be footprints and too straight to be random."

Eli kicked a pebble nervously. "Maybe they're made by Martian worms. You know, big ones. Like, really big ones."

Jack snorted. "Yeah, because worms thrive in freezing temperatures and no air."

Mia smirked. "Don't encourage him, Jack. You know he stayed up all night watching alien movies again."

"I'm just saying," Eli muttered. "It's not like anyone actually knows what's under the ground here."

Well, we do know this used to be a river," Jack said, gesturing at the dried-up channels cutting through the red soil. "Millions of years ago, water flowed here. Now it's just dust."

Mia nodded, staring at the barren landscape. "And whatever made these tracks isn't water. Unless it's ghost water."

Eli gulped. "Can we not?"

The ground gave a faint rumble beneath their feet as if on cue. The three froze.

"Uh… what was that?" Eli asked, his voice shaking.

"Marsquake," Jack said casually. "Totally normal. Mars still has tectonic activity."

"Cool, cool," Eli said, backing up. "Totally normal. No big deal. I love it here. Great vacation spot."

Mia rolled her eyes but couldn't help grinning. "Relax, Eli. If a giant worm pops out, we'll let it eat you first."

CHAPTER 4: THE METALLIC DISCOVERY

The tracks led them to a flat, open plain, where something shiny glinted in the weak sunlight.

"Is that… metal?" Mia asked, running ahead.

Jack picked up a small fragment. "It's not just metal. It's… smooth like it was forged."

Eli peered over Jack's shoulder. "So, either aliens—or we've discovered Mars' hottest new jewelry brand."

"Very funny," Mia said, kneeling to examine the area. "Look at this—these fragments are in a circle. It's like something landed here."

Jack's eyes lit up. "Meteorite. Mars is full of craters from ancient impacts. Some of the metals could've come from that."

Eli picked up another shard. "Or it's alien trash. Like their version of littering."

Really?" Mia asked, raising an eyebrow. "You think aliens traveled light-years just to throw garbage on Mars?"

"I'm just saying, weirder stuff has happened. Like us getting here," Eli retorted.

Before Mia could respond, the ground rumbled again, and a gust of wind blew the red dust away, revealing a circular hatch at the center of the fragments.

"Oh no," Eli said, stepping back. "Nope. Absolutely not. We're not opening that."

"Who said anything about opening it?" Mia asked, grinning. "I'm just going to… investigate."

Jack sighed. "Here we go."

CHAPTER 5: THE HATCH

The metallic hatch gleamed faintly in the Martian sunlight, its surface etched with strange symbols. Mia crouched next to it, her hand hovering above the edges.

"Don't touch it," Eli warned. "This is how every horror movie starts."

"Good thing we're not in a horror movie," Mia said, flashing him a grin. "Besides, we survived the moon, remember?"

"Barely," Eli muttered. "And there weren't mysterious hatches on the moon."

"Just let her do it," Jack said, leaning on a nearby rock. "If it eats her, we'll make a run for it."

Mia rolled her eyes. "You guys are so supportive."

Before Eli could protest further, Mia pressed her hand to the hatch. To their surprise, it began to glow faintly, a greenish-blue light spreading across its surface.

Oh great," Eli groaned. "We've activated the Martian Death Trap."

The hatch slid open with a hiss, revealing a dark tunnel leading into the ground. A faint light flickered at the bottom, casting eerie shadows.

Mia stood, brushing the dust off her hands. "Well, looks like we're going in."

Eli threw his hands up. "Of course we are. Because walking into creepy alien tunnels is always a great idea."

Jack smirked. "You coming or staying out here with the worms?"

Eli groaned but followed them in. "I hate both of you."

CHAPTER 6: THE CHAMBER

The tunnel opened into a massive underground chamber, its walls lined with strange, glowing machinery. The soft hum of the machines filled the air, making the room feel alive.

"Okay, this is… insane," Jack said, staring at the glowing panels. "This isn't natural. This is alien tech."

"Thanks, Captain Obvious," Mia said, stepping closer to the center of the room. "Look at that."

In the middle of the chamber was a pedestal holding a glowing orb that pulsed with green and blue light. The kids stared in awe as images began to flicker across its surface.

"What's it doing?" Eli asked, hiding slightly behind Jack.

"It's showing us something," Jack said. "Look—those are rivers. And lakes."

The orb shifted, displaying a lush, green Mars, its surface covered in water and teeming with life.

"This is what Mars used to look like," Mia whispered. "It's... beautiful."

The orb changed again, showing a vast city with shimmering towers under twin moons.

Jack's jaw dropped. "That's... impossible. Mars had intelligent life?"

"Guess it's not just worms after all," Mia said, smirking at Eli.

"Not funny," Eli muttered. "Also, this feels like a trap."

The orb flickered one last time, displaying a single message in glowing letters:

"Help us restore what was lost."

CHAPTER 7: ESCAPE AND NEW QUESTIONS

Before they could process the message, the room trembled, and the glowing machines began to dim.

"Uh… I think it's time to leave," Eli said, edging toward the tunnel.

"No kidding," Jack said, grabbing Mia's arm. "Let's go!"

The kids sprinted back through the tunnel as the chamber collapsed behind them. They burst out onto the surface, gasping for air as the hatch sealed itself shut.

For a moment, they just stood there, staring at the now-silent plain.

"So," Eli said, breaking the silence. "We're just… not going to talk about that?"

"Talk about what?" Mia asked, grinning. "The alien city? The glowing orb? Or the part where you screamed like a baby?"

I did not scream," Eli said, crossing his arms. "I made a tactical noise of alarm."

Jack chuckled. "Tactical noise. Sure."

Mia looked at the horizon, her smile fading. "Whatever's down there, it needs help. And I don't think this is the last we've heard from Mars."

Eli groaned. "Great. Can't wait for the next adventure."

Jack grinned. "Just admit it—you love it."

"Sure," Eli said, walking toward the rocket. "I love risking my life on alien planets. Totally my thing."

As they climbed back into the rocket, the faint hum began again, and their eyelids grew heavy. Wherever the culvert rocket was taking them next, they knew one thing: life would never be boring.

ACTIVITY 1: WRITING ASSIGNMENT - CREATIVE STORYTELLING

Title: Write Your Own Space Adventure

- **Instructions:**

Imagine you and your friends found a mysterious object in your backyard that could take you to another planet. Write a story about your journey. Be sure to include:

1. Where you travel (it doesn't have to be Mars!).
2. What strange things you discover.
3. How you solve a mystery or problem.
4. Whether or not you return safely—and what happens next!

- **Extension:**

Include drawings of the planet you visited or the mysterious object you found.

ACTIVITY 2: VOCABULARY EXPLORATION

Title: Martian Mystery Vocabulary

• **Instructions:** Match the words to their correct definitions, using what you learned from the story.

Word Definition

1. Atmosphere — a) The outer layer of gases surrounding a planet.

2. Marsquake — b) A term for seismic activity (like earthquakes) on Mars.

3. Meteorite — c) A piece of space rock that lands on a planet's surface.

4. Tectonic Activity — d) Movements in a planet's crust that cause quakes or shifts.

5. Basalt — e) A type of volcanic rock found on Mars and Earth.

6. Hologram — f) A three-dimensional image created with light.

• **Extension Activity:**

Write a sentence for each word, describing how it was used or seen in the story.

ACTIVITY 3: PUZZLES

Puzzle 1: Word Search

Title: Mars Exploration Word Search

Find the following words hidden in the grid:

- Mars, Meteorite, Atmosphere, Tectonic, Mystery, Gravity, Rover, Worm, Orbit, Moon, Rocket, Basalt

WORD SEARCH GRID:

```
M A R S Q U A K E A G
A T R O C K E T M Y B
T O E A M Y S T E R E
E C B A S A L T G R A
O N A W O R M O T S V
R I E O R B I T R E I
I T R E M A R S M O Y
T E C T O N I C T E E
E M O O N R O V E R S
```

Puzzle 2: Mars Crossword

Title: Martian Mystery Crossword

<table>
<tr><td></td><td></td><td></td><td></td><td></td><td>O</td></tr>
<tr><td></td><td></td><td></td><td></td><td></td><td>L</td></tr>
<tr><td></td><td></td><td></td><td></td><td></td><td>Y</td></tr>
<tr><td></td><td></td><td></td><td></td><td></td><td>M</td></tr>
<tr><td></td><td></td><td></td><td></td><td></td><td>P</td></tr>
<tr><td></td><td></td><td></td><td></td><td></td><td>U</td></tr>
<tr><td></td><td></td><td>M</td><td>A</td><td>R</td><td>S</td></tr>
<tr><td></td><td></td><td>N</td><td>O</td><td>O</td><td>M</td></tr>
<tr><td></td><td></td><td></td><td></td><td>V</td><td>O</td></tr>
<tr><td></td><td></td><td></td><td></td><td>E</td><td>N</td></tr>
<tr><td>R</td><td>O</td><td>V</td><td>E</td><td>R</td><td>S</td></tr>
<tr><td></td><td></td><td></td><td>A</td><td></td><td></td></tr>
<tr><td></td><td></td><td></td><td>R</td><td></td><td></td></tr>
<tr><td></td><td></td><td></td><td>T</td><td></td><td></td></tr>
<tr><td></td><td></td><td></td><td>H</td><td></td><td></td></tr>
</table>

Clues:

Across:

1. The fourth planet from the Sun, also known as the Red Planet. (MARS)
2. A robotic explorer sent to study planets. (ROVER)
3. Earth's natural satellite. (MOON)

Down:

1. A robotic vehicle that explores Mars. (ROVER)
2. The planet we live on. (EARTH)
3. The tallest volcano in the solar system, found on Mars. (OLYMPUS MONS)

ACTIVITY 4: QUIZ

Title: Martian Mystery Quiz

1. What is a Marsquake?

    a) A storm on Mars.
    b) Seismic activity on Mars.
    c) The movement of Mars' atmosphere.

2. What caused the tracks the kids followed?

    a) A giant Martian worm.
    b) A dried-up riverbed.
    c) The trail of a meteorite fragment.

3. Why is Mars called the "Red Planet"?

    a) Its rocks contain iron that turns red when it rusts.
    b) Its sunsets are always red.
    c) Mars has volcanoes that glow red.

4. What is basalt, and why is it important on Mars?

    a) A type of Martian plant.
    b) Volcanic rock that shows Mars' volcanic past.
    c) A rare mineral that makes Mars glow red.

5. **True or False:** The kids discovered evidence of an ancient Martian city.

ACTIVITY 5: LOGIC PUZZLE - WHO TOOK WHAT?

Title: Mars Mystery: Who Found What?

Mia, Eli, and Jack each discovered something unique on Mars. Use the clues to figure out who found what, how they found it, and how long it took.

Clues:

1. Mia's discovery took the longest to find and was buried under the most dust.
2. Eli didn't find the metallic fragments.
3. Jack found his discovery in just 10 minutes.
4. The glowing orb was uncovered using a brush.
5. Mia didn't use the magnetic tool.

Chart to fill in:

Name	Discovery	Tools Used	Time Taken
Mia			
Eli			
Jack			

ACTIVITY 6: CREATIVE DRAWING

Title: Design Your Own Mars Artifact

• **Instructions:** Imagine you're exploring Mars and discover an artifact left behind by an ancient Martian civilization. Draw your artifact and label its parts. Write a short paragraph explaining what it does, who might have made it, and why it was left on Mars.

This collection of activities combines writing, puzzles, vocabulary, and quizzes to engage students with the story's themes while reinforcing knowledge about Mars. Let me know if you'd like further customizations!

Martian Mystery Story & Activities
The Martian Mystery: Mia, Eli, and Jack's Adventure
Chapter 1: The Culvert Rocket
Two weeks had passed since Mia, Eli, and Jack returned from their unbelievable journey to the moon. No one at school would believe them, of course. How could they? The trio had built their spaceship from an old culvert they found in the woods...
(Include all expanded story chapters here as written.)
Educational Activities

Activity 1: Writing Assignment - Creative Storytelling

Imagine you and your friends found a mysterious object in your backyard that could take you to another planet. Write a story about your journey. Be sure to include where you travel, what you discover, how you solve a mystery, and what happens next.

Martian Mystery Story & Activities
Activity 4: Extended Quiz and Answer Sheet

Activity 4: Extended Quiz - Martian Mystery

1. What is a Marsquake?
    a) A storm on Mars
    b) Seismic activity on Mars
    c) The movement of Mars' atmosphere
      Answer: ___________

2. What caused the tracks the kids followed?
    a) A giant Martian worm
    b) A dried-up riverbed
    c) The trail of a meteorite fragment
      Answer: ___________

3. Why is Mars called the "Red Planet"?
    a) Its rocks contain iron that turns red when it rusts
    b) Its sunsets are always red
    c) Mars has volcanoes that glow red
      Answer: ___________

4. What is basalt, and why is it important on Mars?
    a) A type of Martian plant
    Martian Mystery Story & Activities
    b) Volcanic rock that shows Mars' volcanic past
    c) A rare mineral that makes Mars glow red
      Answer: ___________

5. True or False: The kids discovered evidence of an ancient Martian city.
      Answer: ___________

6. (Essay Question) Describe how the kids solved the
   mystery of the moving rocks on Mars. Use examples from the story
   to explain their process and how they worked as a team.
   Answer:

____

____

____

____

____

7. (Essay Question) Imagine you're an astronaut on Mars.
   What would be the three most important tools or equipment you
   would take, and why?
   Answer:

____

____

____

____

____

ANSWER KEY FOR ALL ACTIVITIES

1. Vocabulary Matching:

Atmosphere: a) The outer layer of gases surrounding a planet.

Marsquake: b) Seismic activity on Mars.

Meteorite: c) A piece of space rock that lands on a planet's surface.

Tectonic Activity: d) Movements in a planet's crust that cause quakes or shifts.

Basalt: e) A type of volcanic rock found on Mars and Earth.

Hologram: f) A three-dimensional image created with light.

2. Quiz:

1. b) Seismic activity on Mars
2. c) The trail of a meteorite fragment
3. a) Its rocks contain iron that turns red when it rusts
4. b) Volcanic rock that shows Mars' volcanic past
5. True

3. Essay Answers: (Example only, student-specific answers expected)

Essay on teamwork: The kids used scientific reasoning and tools like observation, deduction, and collaboration to solve the mystery of the moving rocks. Mia's leadership, Jack's technical knowledge, and Eli's cautious approach all contributed.

Astronaut equipment: Answers will vary but may include items like oxygen tanks, rovers, and scientific instruments.

www.ingramcontent.com/pod-product-compliance
Lightning Source LLC
Chambersburg PA
CBHW071444300726
48976CB00004B/1437